Jeet and Fudge

THE DUELING LEMONADE STANDS

by Amandeep S. Kochar

PAW PRINTS PUBLISHING

pawprintspublishing.com

Glossary

Bapu (baa-poo): *Dad* in Punjabi

Bebbe (beb-be): *Mom* in Punjabi

Sewa (say-va): selfless service

Patka (pat-kuh): a piece of cloth that covers the head; worn by Sikh boys

Dasvandh: The donation of a tenth of one's income for charitable causes

This is a work of fiction. Names, characters, places, and incidents either are the product of the author's imagination or are used fictitiously. Any resemblance to actual persons, living or dead, events, or locales is entirely coincidental.

Copyright © 2023 by Paw Prints Publishing

All rights reserved. No part of this book may be reproduced or used in any matter without written permission of the copyright owner except for the use of quotations in a book review.

Book and Cover Design by Maureen O'Connor
Art Direction by Nishant Mudgal
Illustrated by Weaverbird Interactive
Edited by Bobbie Bensur and Alison A. Curtin

English Paperback ISBN: 978-1-22318-761-7
English Library ISBN: 978-1-22318-760-0
English eBook ISBN: 978-1-22318-762-4

Published by Paw Prints Publishing
PawPrintsPublishing.com
Printed in Canada

It is hot today!

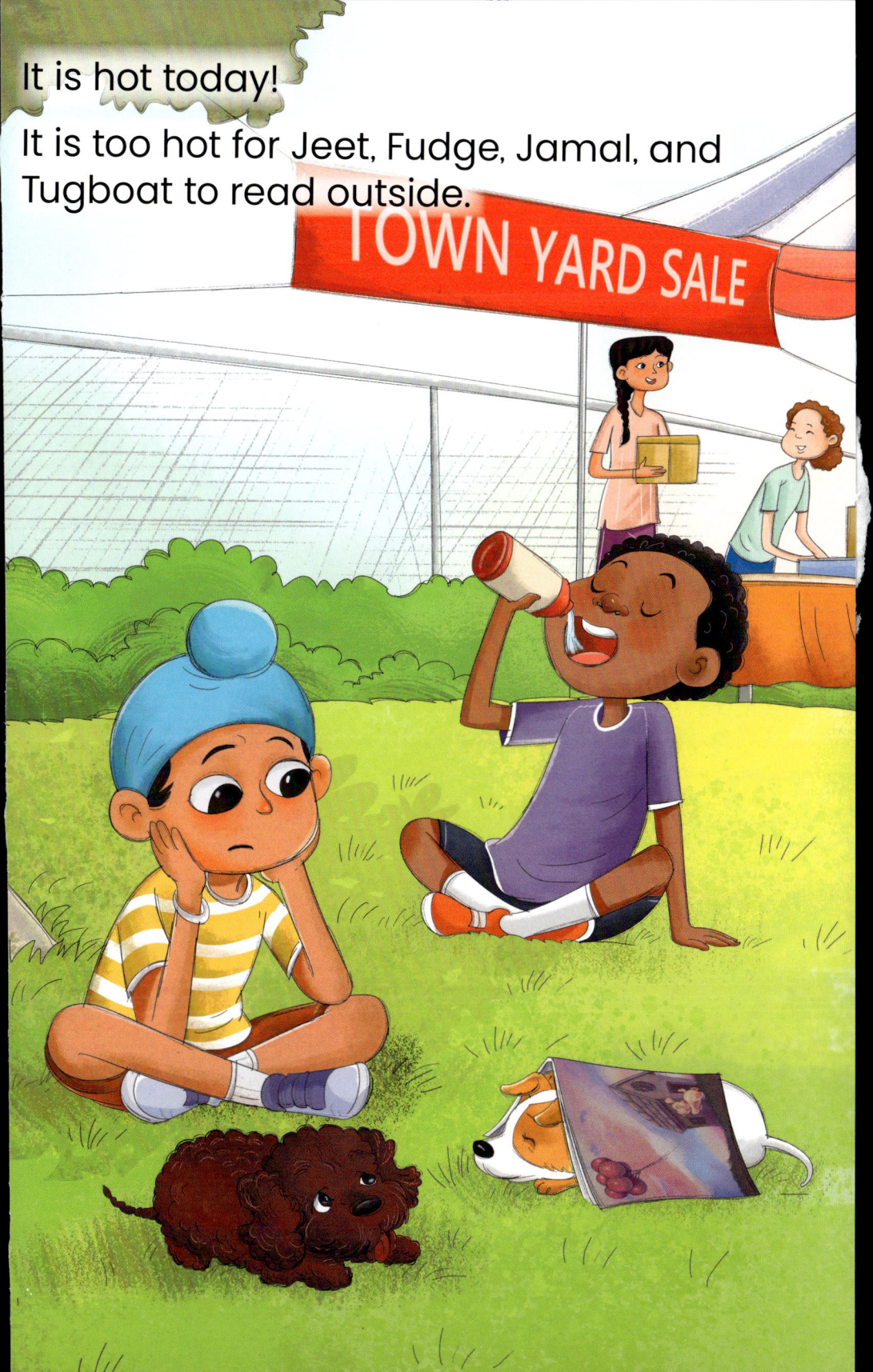

It is too hot for Jeet, Fudge, Jamal, and Tugboat to read outside.

TOWN YARD SALE

The pool is too crowded.

The line for ice cream is too long.

The puppies at the shelter are too sluggish to play.

"It is so hot," says Jeet. "These puppies need a fan!"

"Woof! Woof!" Fudge and Tugboat agree.

"You could raise money to buy a solar-powered fan!" says Dad.

"I have an idea," says Jeet.

The friends get to work. They find:

A folding table, a basket, plastic cups, water, sugar,

and lemons!

A lot of lemons!

"A lemonade stand! Good idea, Jeet."

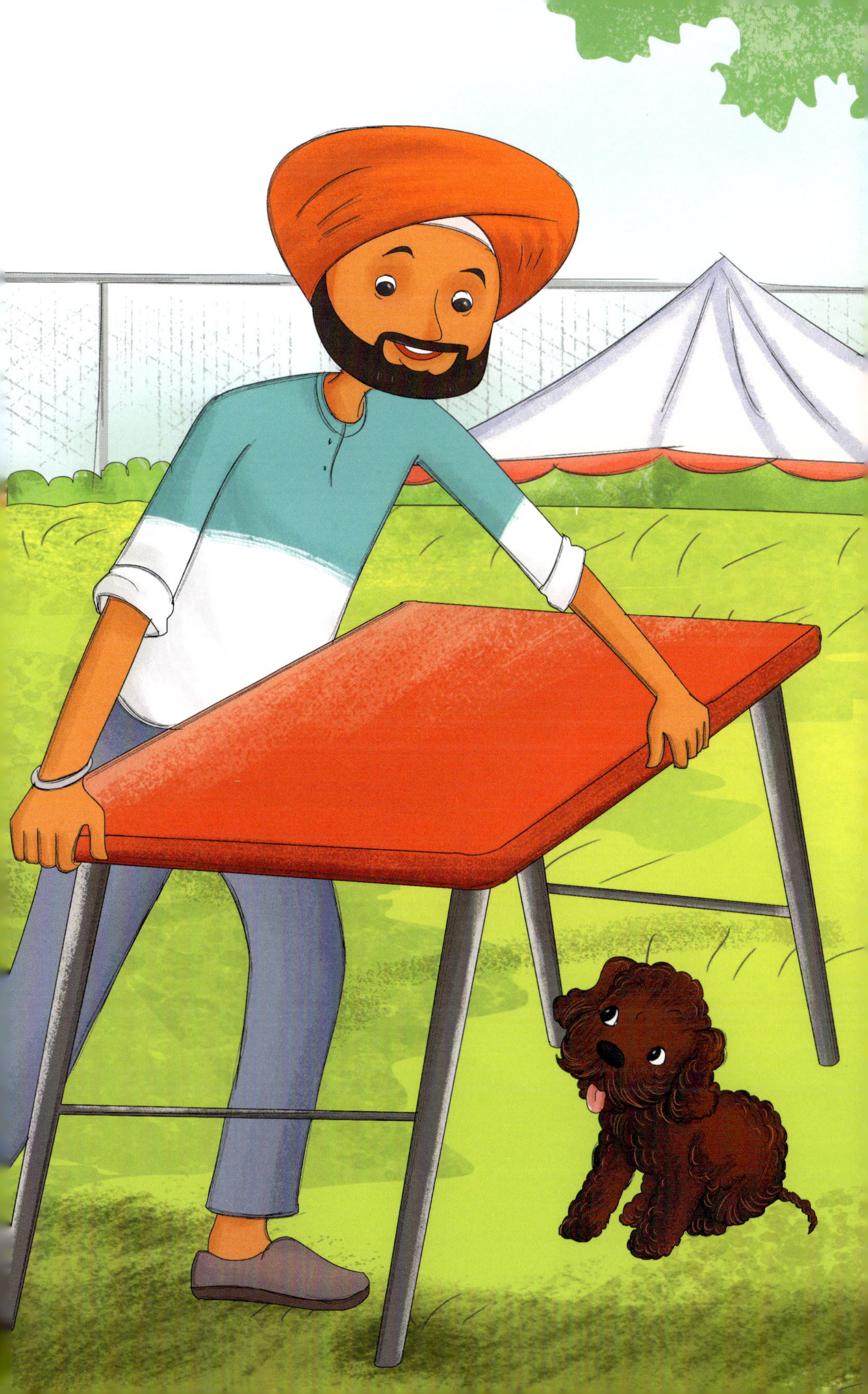

The four friends sell *a lot* of lemonade.
Everyone *loves* lemonade on a hot day!

Uh-oh!

Looks like there is competition!

Pink Lemonade

"Hey! We were here first," says Jamal.

"So? There's room for both stands! I am Mary and this is Lola, by the way."

"And this is Fluffy and Scout."

Hmppfff...

Pink Lemonade

Lemonade

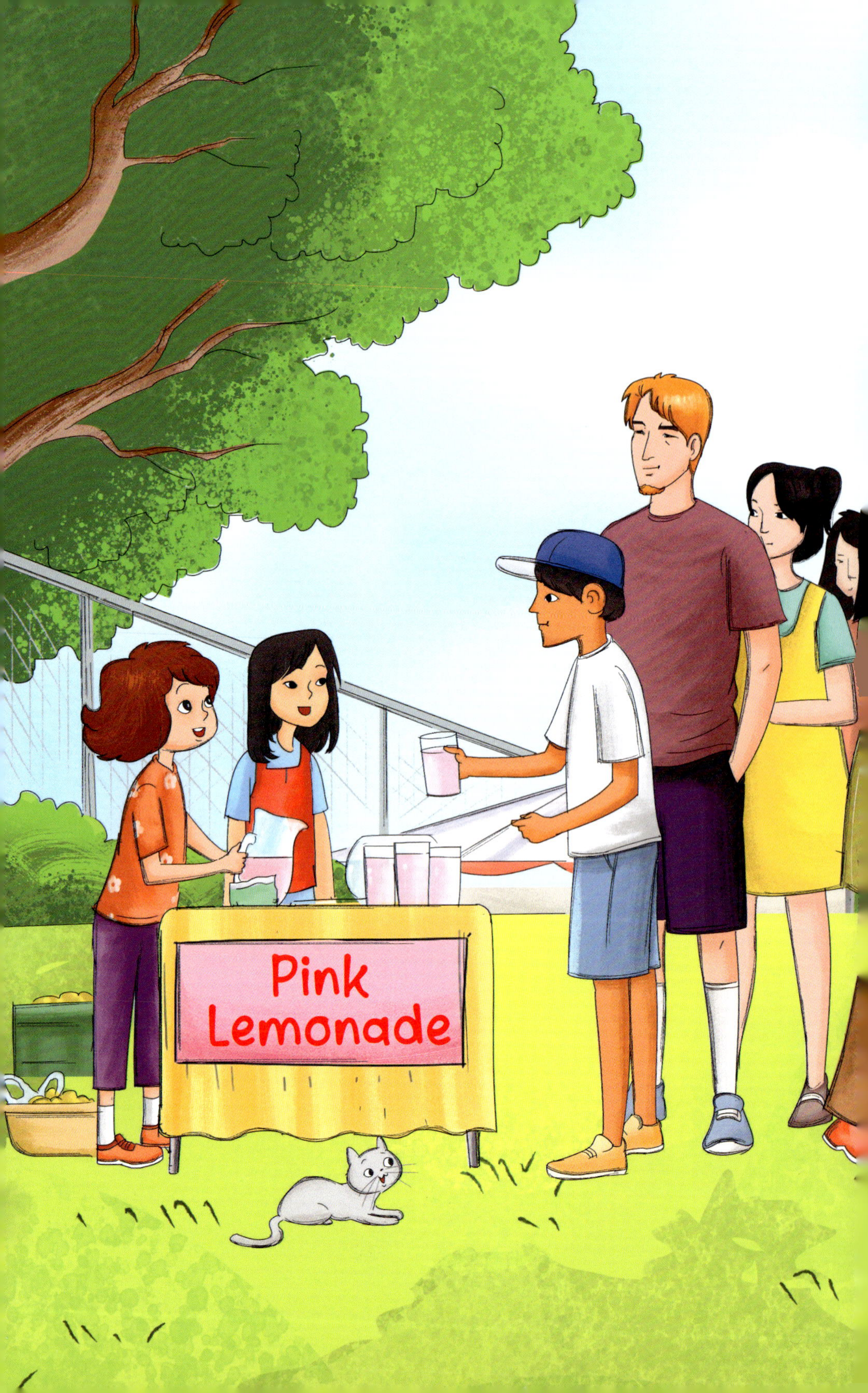
Pink
Lemonade

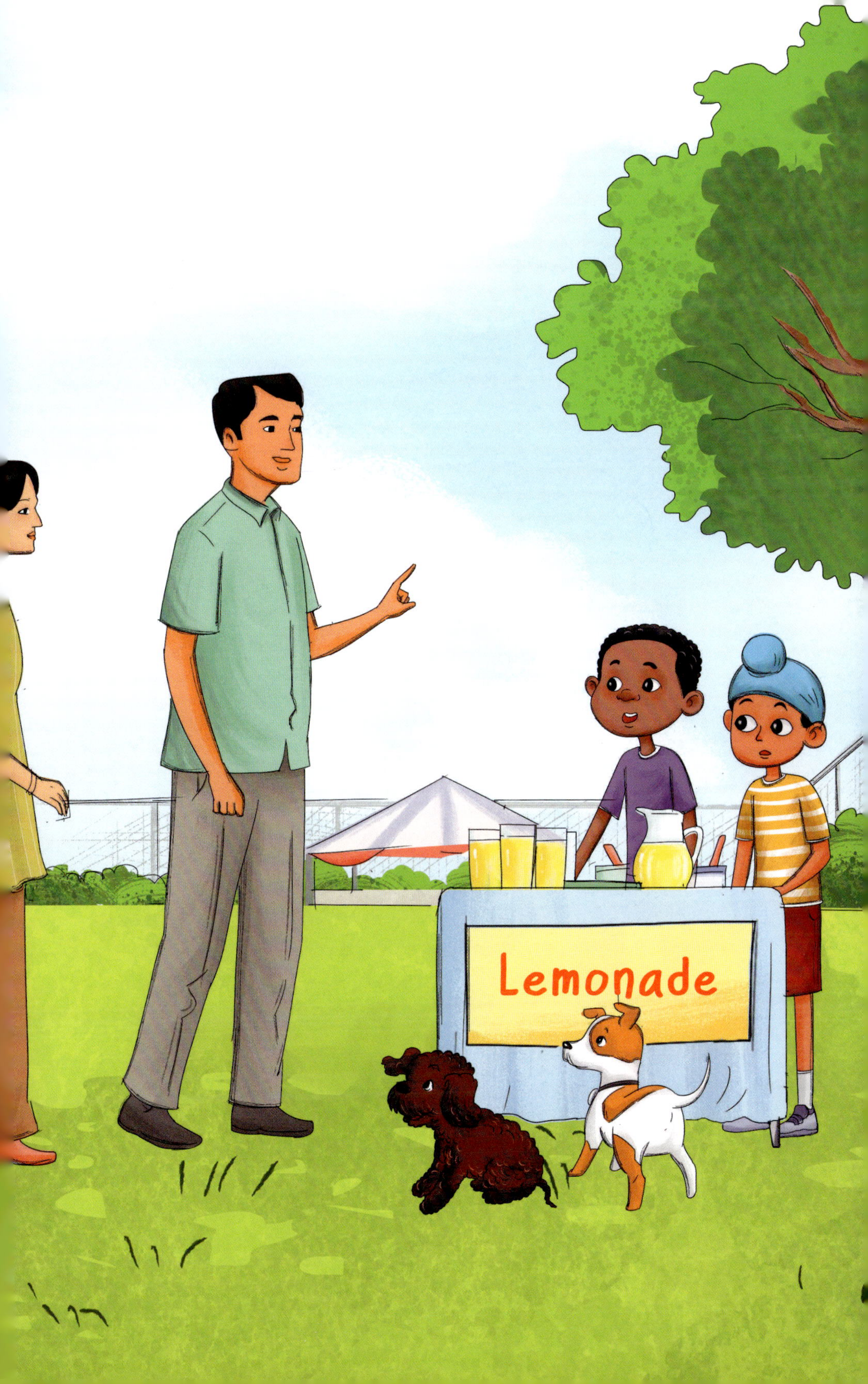
Lemonade

"See?" says Mary. "We send people to your table if they like *yellow* lemonade. We sell them ours if they like *pink!*"

"That is nice. Thank you!" says Jeet.

"We are going to buy a fan for the puppies at the shelter."

"We are trying to buy a fan too! For our grandma. She plays chess at the rec center."

"You are *sisters*?"

"Yes! I was adopted," says Lola.

"I was adopted, too! High five for forever families and forever friends!"

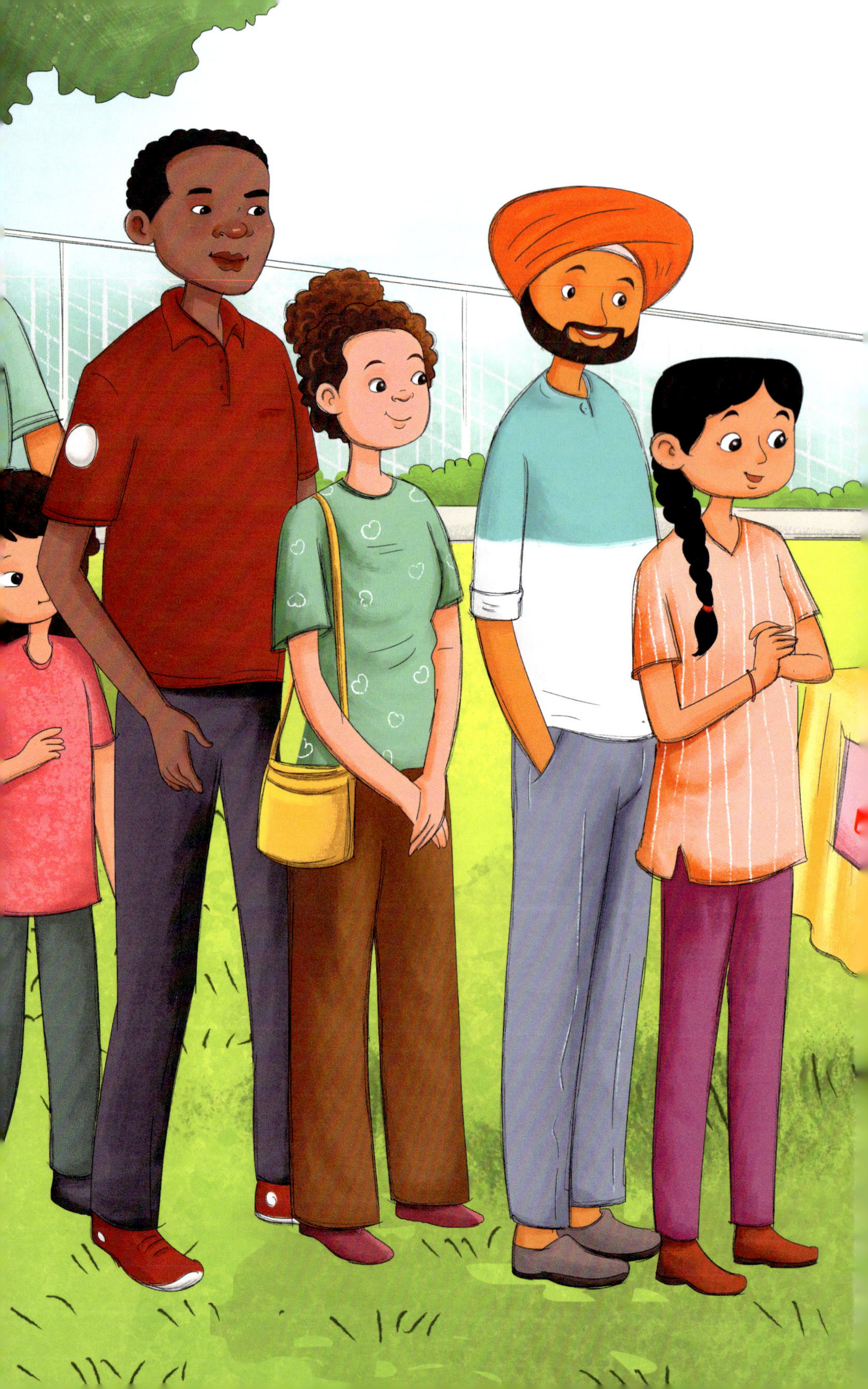

"Come on! Let's do this together," says Jamal. "We'll get both of those fans!"

"It looks like we have some new forever friends! Huh, Fudge?"

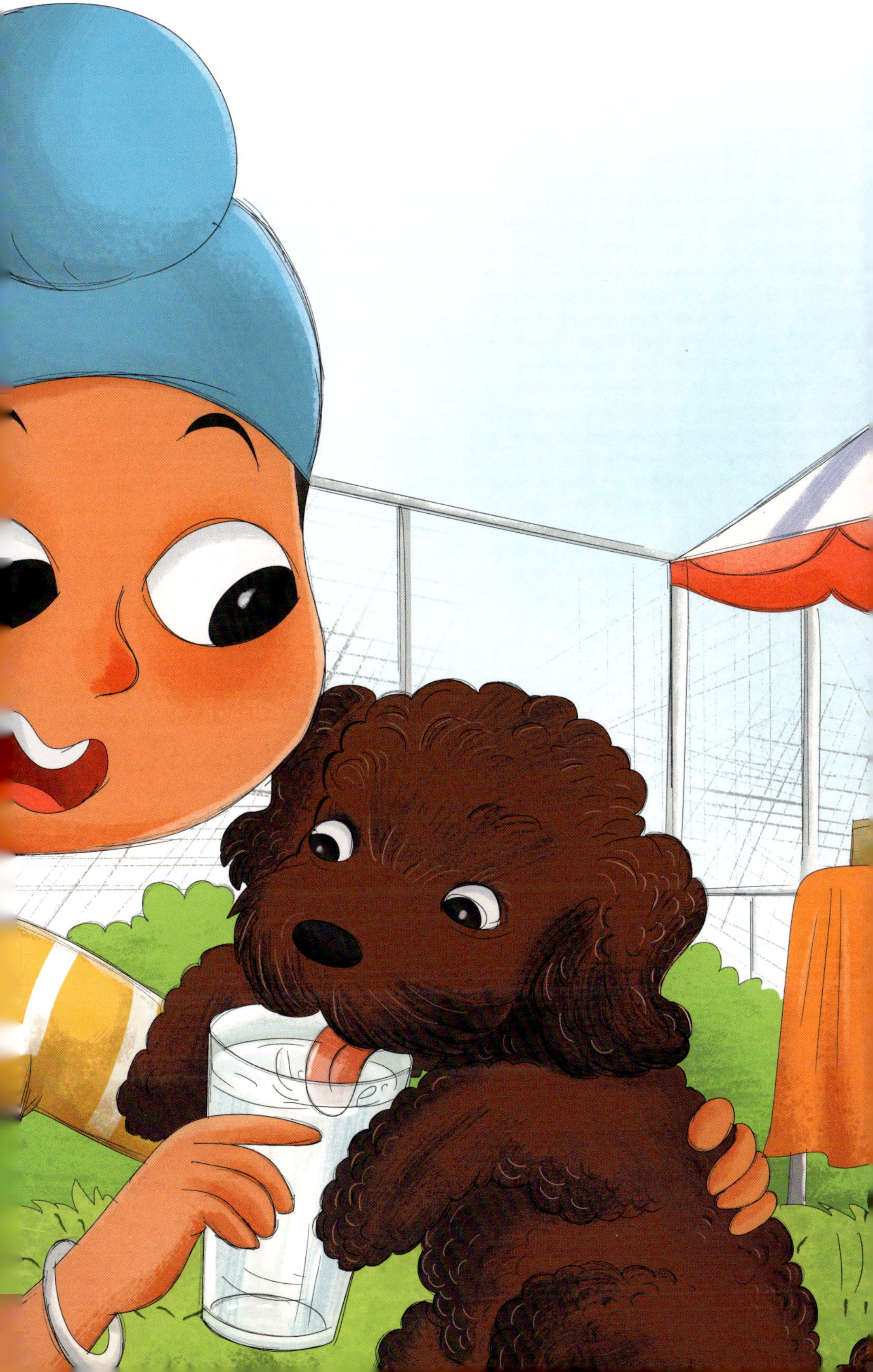

Finding a common cause to support is a great way for kids to feel empowered and connect with one another. Parents and caregivers can help, too!

The time kids spend volunteering or working toward a goal (like raising money at a lemonade stand for their local animal shelter or rec center) can increase their empathy and compassion for others. Studies show kids that do these types of activities early on in life build charitable habits and compassion that can last a lifetime!

In Jeet and Fudge: *The Dueling Lemonade Stands*, Jeet and Jamal, and Mary and Lola decide to sell lemonade for different community causes. Ultimately, rather than try to compete, all four kids come to realize that the best way to achieve their goals is by working together. Helping others is what unites them!

And that's not all that unites them. All four characters – Jeet, Jamal, Mary, and Lola – have either been adopted or care about someone who has been adopted. The kids in this story all come from different backgrounds, yet they have a few very important things in common.

In Sikhism, the religion Jeet and his family practice, the concept of selfless charitable giving and charitable work is called *sewa*. And should Jeet donate at least 10% of his lemonade stand earnings to a good cause, that is called *Dasvandh*. This word means sharing what you have, or part of what you have earned, to help others. Other religions worldwide follow a similar principle.

What unites you and your friends? What empowers you? What do you want to do to give back to your community?